STAR WARS

THE CLONE WARS

Adapted by Rob Valois

Based on the movie *Star Wars: The Clone Wars*

Grosset & Dunlap • LucasBooks

THE BATTLE BEGINS

GROSSET & DUNLAP
Published by the Penguin Group
Penguin Group (USA) Inc., 375 Hudson Street, New York, New York 10014, USA
Penguin Group (Canada), 90 Eglinton Avenue East, Suite 700, Toronto, Ontario M4P 2Y3, Canada
(a division of Pearson Penguin Canada Inc.)
Penguin Books Ltd., 80 Strand, London WC2R 0RL, England
Penguin Group Ireland, 25 St. Stephen's Green, Dublin 2, Ireland
(a division of Penguin Books Ltd.)
Penguin Group (Australia), 250 Camberwell Road, Camberwell, Victoria 3124, Australia
(a division of Pearson Australia Group Pty. Ltd.)
Penguin Books India Pvt. Ltd., 11 Community Centre, Panchsheel Park, New Delhi—110 017, India
Penguin Group (NZ), 67 Apollo Drive, Rosedale, North Shore 0632, New Zealand
(a division of Pearson New Zealand Ltd.)
Penguin Books (South Africa) (Pty.) Ltd., 24 Sturdee Avenue,
Rosebank, Johannesburg 2196, South Africa

Penguin Books Ltd., Registered Offices:
80 Strand, London WC2R 0RL, England

This book is published in partnership with LucasBooks, a division of Lucasfilm Ltd.

Library of Congress Cataloging-in-Publication Data is available.

ISBN: 978-0-448-44991-3   10 9 8 7 6 5 4 3 2

For over a thousand generations, the Jedi Knights have been the guardians of peace
and justice in the Galactic Republic.

Recruited from all over the galaxy, the members of the Jedi Order are trained in the use of the mystical energy known as the Force.

"The Force is what gives a Jedi his power. It's an energy field created by all living things. It surrounds us, penetrates us, and binds the galaxy together." —Jedi Master Obi-Wan Kenobi

The Jedi use the power of the Force to maintain order throughout the galaxy. They believe in harmony and compassion.

Their mortal enemy, the Sith, follow the dark side of the Force, which is fueled by hate and anger. They are determined to defeat the Jedi and steal control of the galaxy.

The Republic has fallen into civil war. The evil Sith Lord Count Dooku and his Separatist Alliance are attempting to seize control of the galaxy. To defend the Republic, Supreme Chancellor Palpatine, the head of the Republic, has committed thousands of clone troopers to the battle.

The wise Jedi Master Obi-Wan Kenobi is a high-ranking general in the clone army. Disciplined and courageous, he fights to preserve the Republic.

By his side is his former student, the headstrong Jedi Knight Anakin Skywalker. Brash and young, Skywalker still has a lot to learn from his old Master.

On the planet Christophsis, the Jedi lead the Republic forces against the Separatists' massive droid army.

Only the Jedi generals and an army of clone troopers stand between Dooku and the downfall of the Republic.

Genetically created and raised on the planet of Kamino, the clone troopers are identical soldiers who were bred to serve the Republic. They have been trained since birth to become the most efficient military force in the galaxy.

Unlike the clones, the Separatist Army is made up of many different types of battle droids. Two of their main attack models are the octuptarra droid and the spider droid.

Their rotating bodies allow the droids to change direction almost instantly, and their weapons can fire over long distances, making them almost impossible to destroy . . . unless you are a Jedi.

The battle on Christophsis has taken its toll on the Republic forces. The Jedi generals and the clone troopers are in desperate need of help and are expecting the return of a cruiser full of reinforcements.

However, instead of a fresh batch of clone troopers and supplies, the Republic cruiser delivers a small Togruta girl to them.

"I'm Ahsoka Tano," the young girl says. "Master Yoda sent me."

Yoda needs Obi-Wan and Anakin for an important mission, but the two Jedi won't leave until Christophsis is secure.

"I'm the new Padawan learner," she says, honored to be in the presence of the two Jedi.

"And I'm Obi-Wan Kenobi, your new Master."

"I'm at your service, Master Kenobi," she replies, "but I'm afraid that I've actually been assigned to Master Skywalker."

Anakin's eyes light up in shock. "What?! No, no, no, no, no, no!" he shouts. "There must be some mistake!"

But there is no mistake. Master Yoda was very specific: Ahsoka is to be Anakin's Padawan.

With the battle raging on, the young Jedi has no choice but to take his apprentice along.

This is Ahsoka's first adventure and she is eager to prove herself to her new Master.

And while she does prove herself to be a worthy student and assists in winning the battle on Christophsis, Anakin finds some of her methods to be troubling.

"You're reckless, little one," Anakin addresses his student. "You never would have made it as Obi-Wan's Padawan, but you might make it as mine."

With the battle on Christophsis over, Obi-Wan, Anakin, and Ahsoka can finally get to Yoda's important mission.

On the desert planet of Tatooine, Obi-Wan Kenobi meets with crime lord Jabba the Hutt. Jabba's son has been kidnapped, and in order to obtain a treaty for safe passage through Hutt Space, the Jedi have agreed to help find the Huttlet.

Obi-Wan stands before the powerful Jabba. "We will not let you down," the Jedi says.

"AHHH . . . WOWOGA SLEEMO MAKA PEEDUNKEE MUFKIN," the Hutt replies.

His protocol droid, TC-70, translates. "The most gracious Jabba has one more small
condition. He demands you bring back the slime who kidnapped his little . . . punky muffin."

Anakin Skywalker, Ahsoka, and **R2-D2** arrive on the planet of Teth located in the Outer Rim of the galaxy. The Jedi discover that the Huttlet is being held captive in an old Hutt castle.

However, it appears that the Jedi aren't the only ones interested in Jabba's son. A mysterious hooded figure is recording their every move. On Tatooine, Dooku meets with Jabba.

"Oh, great Jabba the Hutt, I have news of your son. I have discovered that it is the Jedi who have captured him."

But before Anakin and Ahsoka can get the Huttlet to safety, they are confronted by the assassin Asajj Ventress. Trained in the dark side, she is a formidable opponent, even for the most powerful Jedi.

Barely escaping the clutches of Ventress, the Jedi make their way through the castle and toward the landing strip where a Republic gunship will take the Huttlet back to Jabba.

But the Huttlet appears sick and is getting worse by the moment. If Anakin and Ahsoka
don't move quickly, the small Hutt might not make it.

Luck may be on their side. The Republic gunship pulls through the clouds as Anakin and Ahsoka make their way to the rendezvous point.

As Anakin, Ahsoka, and Artoo hurry toward the gunship, the shadow of an oncoming vulture droid fills the sky. The clones try to fight off the droid, but are unable to prevent it from destroying the Republic gunship.

Obi-Wan arrives on Teth to aid Anakin and Ahsoka, but when he gets there he senses an old foe: Ventress.

"Ventress, I can feel your frustration. Let me guess, you're after Jabba's young son, too."

On Tatooine, the Hutt demands an update from Count Dooku, who has now pledged to rescue the Huttlet.

"I can assure you, Jabba, my droid armies are on the verge of defeating the Jedi Skywalker and rescuing your precious heir."

But the Hutt will not discuss a treaty with Dooku until his son is returned.

With their transport ship destroyed, Anakin and Ahsoka must find another way to get the Huttlet home. On a distant, old landing pad they find a beat-up freighter, the *Twilight*. This hunk of junk could be their only way off of Teth.

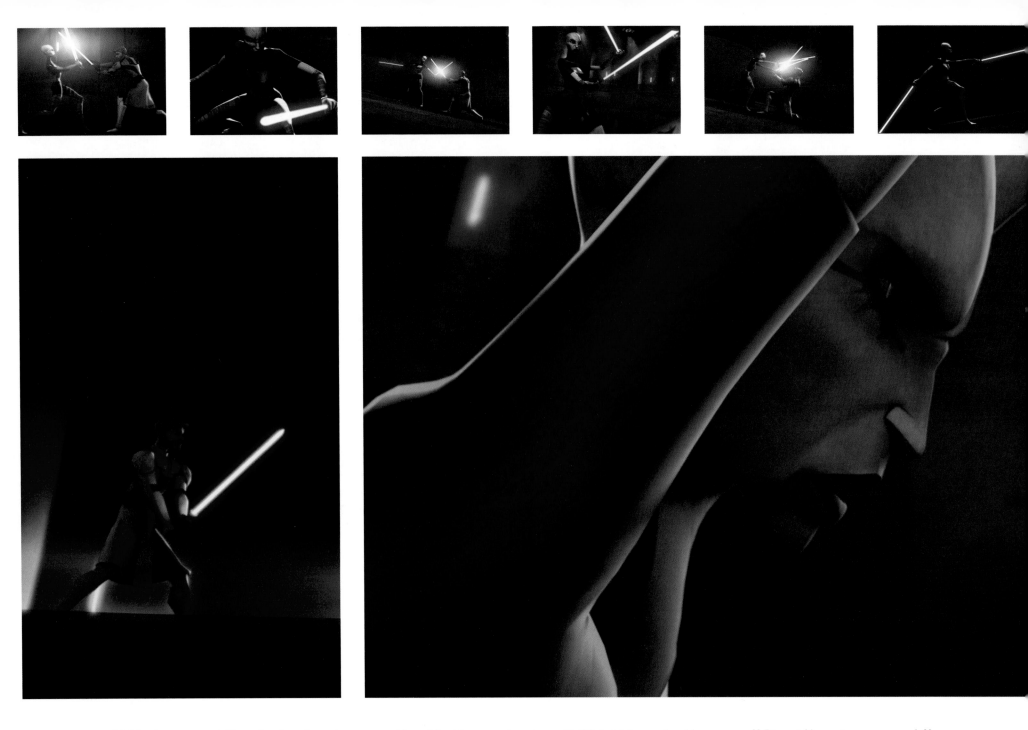

"We know of Dooku's plot to turn the Hutts against us," Obi-Wan challenges. "It will not succeed."

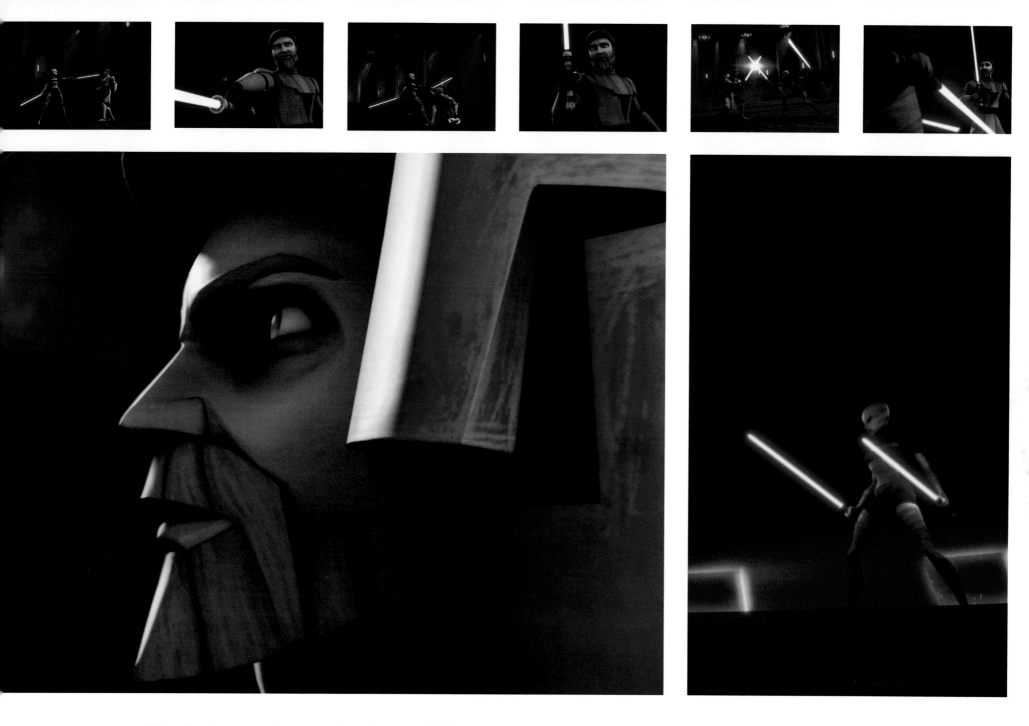

The dark assassin just laughs it off. "It will when the truth dies with you."

Aboard the freighter, Ahsoka is finally able to treat the Huttlet's sickness. With him feeling better, they're off to Tatooine to return him to Jabba. After several failed attempts and some handiwork from Artoo, the *Twilight* finally makes the leap into hyperspace.

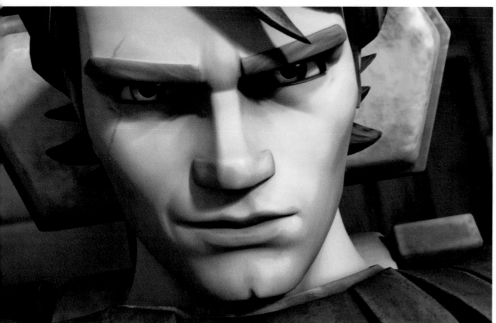

As they drop out of hyperdrive above Tatooine, a MagnaGuard fighter appears. An old freighter is no match for a droid-piloted fighter, but with Artoo at the guns they manage to escape.

However, even Anakin's piloting abilities can't prevent the *Twilight* from taking some damage, and they are forced to make an emergency crash landing in the deserts of Tatooine.

Back at Jabba's palace, Count Dooku reveals the next part of his scheme. He tells the Hutt that Anakin has killed the Huttlet.

"The Jedi plot is quite clear now. They only promised to rescue your son to win your trust. Now Skywalker is coming here to finish his true mission, to wipe out the entire Hutt clan."

On the Republic capital of Coruscant, Chancellor Palpatine and Yoda receive a holographic message from Obi-Wan Kenobi.

"Anakin has reached Tatooine with the Huttlet, Master, but he's still in grave danger. Separatist troops are desperate to intercept him. I think the whole plot was engineered by Dooku to convince Jabba we kidnapped his son."

Yoda responds, "If believe this the Hutts do, ended will our chance of a treaty with them be. Join Dooku and the Separatists Jabba will."

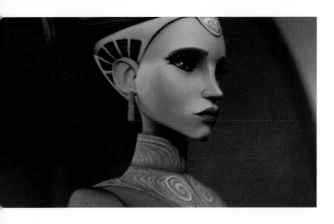

Yoda rises to leave the room as Senator Padmé Amidala enters the chamber.

"Jabba the Hutt has an uncle in the old downtown area here on Coruscant," she offers. "Perhaps I can reason with him and reopen negotiations."

"This is far too dangerous," Palpatine pleads with Padmé. "I beg you, please reconsider this."

"Don't worry, Chancellor, I've dealt with far worse than the Hutts."

Stranded in the middle of the vast Dune Sea of Tatooine, Anakin, Ahsoka, and Artoo must fight the heat and sand to get the Huttlet back home. They decide to split up.

The old downtown sector of Coruscant is the home of Ziro the Hutt and his opulent fifty-story palace. As Padmé arrives, she is led to his throne room by a pair of fierce-looking sentry droids.

She approaches the giant Hutt and says, "I was hoping that you and I could resolve this dispute and broker a treaty between the Republic and the great clan of the Hutts."

"A treaty is impossible," Ziro replies. "My nephew, Jabba's son, has been kidnapped by Jedi scum."

"But, sir," she pleads. "There has been a misunderstanding."

"There is no misunderstanding," the Hutt bellows. "Escort her out!"

But as Padmé is being escorted from Ziro's palace she sees something interesting: Ziro talking with a hologram of Count Dooku.

"Your plot is coming apart, Count Dooku! A Senator from the Republic was here! What if she finds out that I helped you kidnap Jabba's son?"

"Don't worry," Dooku says. "I have convinced Jabba that the Jedi murdered his son and are on their way to kill him."

Ziro replies, "Jabba will murder the Jedi on sight!"

While Padmé is listening, she is caught and stunned by one of the sentry droids.

As Dooku is finishing his conversation with Ziro, he is alerted to Anakin's presence on Tatooine. He leaves to intercept him and when the two meet in the desert, a great battle commences.

"Your training has come a long way, boy," the Sith Lord taunts. "Ah, now I remember, this was your home planet, wasn't it? I sense your strong feelings. Feelings of pain. Loss."

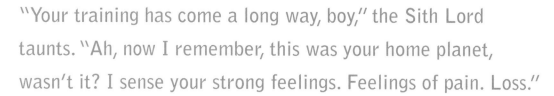

Outside Jabba's palace, Ahsoka and Artoo battle three MagnaGuard droids. They are so close to getting the Huttlet home, but the droids are just too much for them.

Luckily, without the guards knowing, Padmé is able to send a distress message to her loyal droid C-3PO, and before Ziro knows what is happening, a platoon of Republic shock troopers charge into his throne room and free the senator.

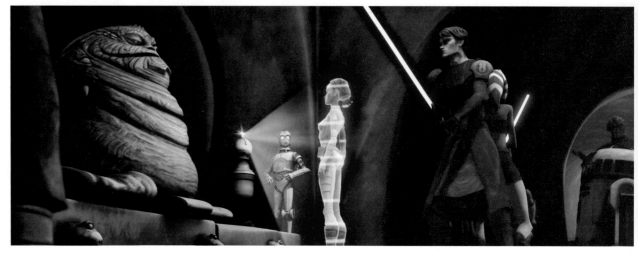

Back on Tatooine, Anakin arrives in Jabba's throne room. Moments later Ahsoka and Artoo join him, after barely escaping from the MagnaGuard droids. They have the Huttlet, and he's still alive. Jabba is thrilled to see his boy, however he still plans to execute the Jedi. A message comes in. It's Padmé.

"Greetings, honorable Jabba. I am Senator Amidala of the Galactic Congress. I have discovered a plot against you by one of your own. Your uncle will admit he conspired with Count Dooku to kidnap your son and frame the Jedi for the crime."

"WAHHH! JANAGA ZIRO KEEZ!" hollers the giant Hutt.

"Ziro will be dealt with by the Hutt family," his droid translates, "most severely."

With the Huttlet safely returned, and the treaty with the Hutts in place, the Jedi can take a moment to enjoy their victory. However, they are constantly aware that new threats from the Sith lie around every corner. The Republic may have won this battle, but the Clone Wars rage on.